NIGHT GARDEN
Poems from the World of Dreams

by JANET S. WONG

illustrated
by JULIE PASCHKIS

MARGARET K. McELDERRY BOOKS

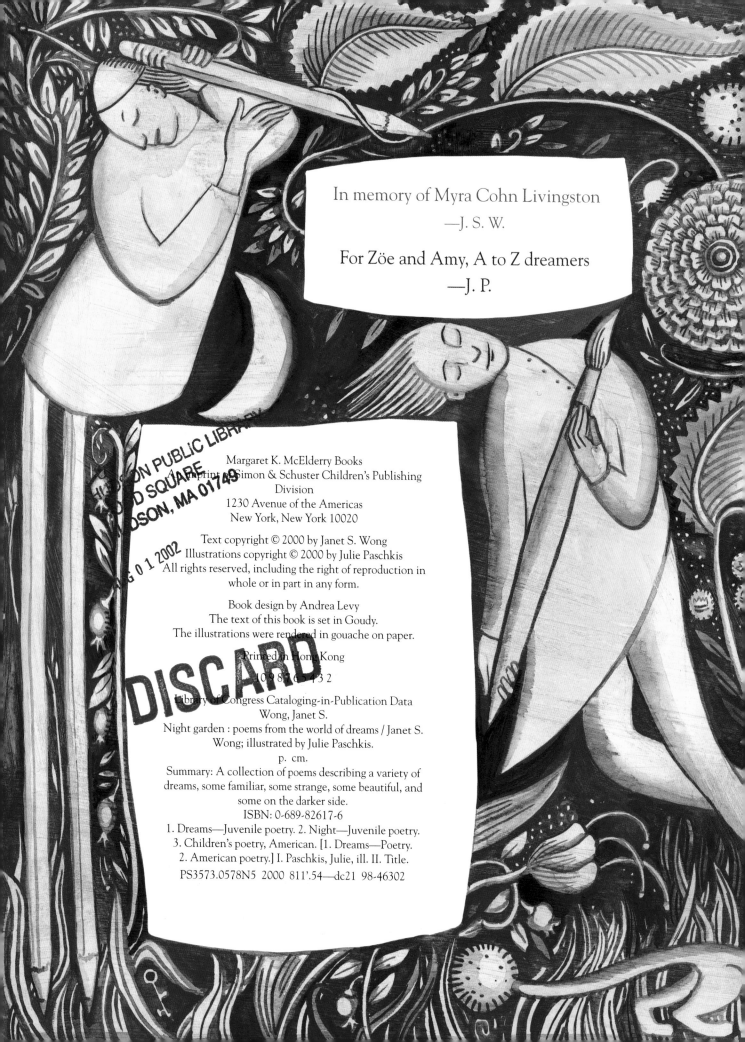

In memory of Myra Cohn Livingston
—J. S. W.

For Zöe and Amy, A to Z dreamers
—J. P.

Margaret K. McElderry Books
An imprint of Simon & Schuster Children's Publishing
Division
1230 Avenue of the Americas
New York, New York 10020

Text copyright © 2000 by Janet S. Wong
Illustrations copyright © 2000 by Julie Paschkis
All rights reserved, including the right of reproduction in
whole or in part in any form.

Book design by Andrea Levy
The text of this book is set in Goudy.
The illustrations were rendered in gouache on paper.

Printed in Hong Kong
10 9 8 7 6 5 4 3 2

Library of Congress Cataloging-in-Publication Data
Wong, Janet S.
Night garden : poems from the world of dreams / Janet S.
Wong; illustrated by Julie Paschkis.
p. cm.
Summary: A collection of poems describing a variety of
dreams, some familiar, some strange, some beautiful, and
some on the darker side.
ISBN: 0-689-82617-6
1. Dreams—Juvenile poetry. 2. Night—Juvenile poetry.
3. Children's poetry, American. [1. Dreams—Poetry.
2. American poetry.] I. Paschkis, Julie, ill. II. Title.
PS3573.0578N5 2000 811'.54—dc21 98-46302

CONTENTS

Night Garden

Deep in the earth
a tangle of roots
sends up
green shoots
and dreams grow
wild,
dreams grow wild
like dandelion weeds,
feathery heads
alive
with seeds—

and these fine seeds,
about to sprout,
race the day
to find their place
in a welcome mind,
in an open space
in a lonely bed—

and they send down roots,
and they sprout
and bloom—

in the night garden.

Whose Face Is This?

I do not recognize
these eyes.
The smile is brighter
than my own.
This hair is not the same
thin hair
that flattens
in the morning air.
Whose face is this
I see tonight?
Is this the face I wear
inside
my skin,
behind the mask
you see?
Whose face is this?
Can it be me?

The Ones They Loved the Most

My mother says
the spirits of the dead
visit
in dreams,
seeking out
the ones they loved
the most.
When you are chosen,
remember to pull
at the air around you
when you wake,
pull and gulp it down,
swallow hard,
and those sweet memories
will stick
like cotton candy.

Old Friend

I had forgotten you, friend.
Is that why you came
into my dream?
I had forgotten you.

When I fall asleep again,
will you leave your address
on my pillow?

Who Knows How Long

A stranger asks me something
in French
and I answer,
Oui, c'est vrai,
even while I am thinking in my sleep
this cannot be,
to say more than I know
in French so fast it runs off my tongue,
flies out my mouth
the way a goose flies south for winter,

the way a goose flies south,
by instinct,
some knowledge wedged deep in her heart
who knows how long.

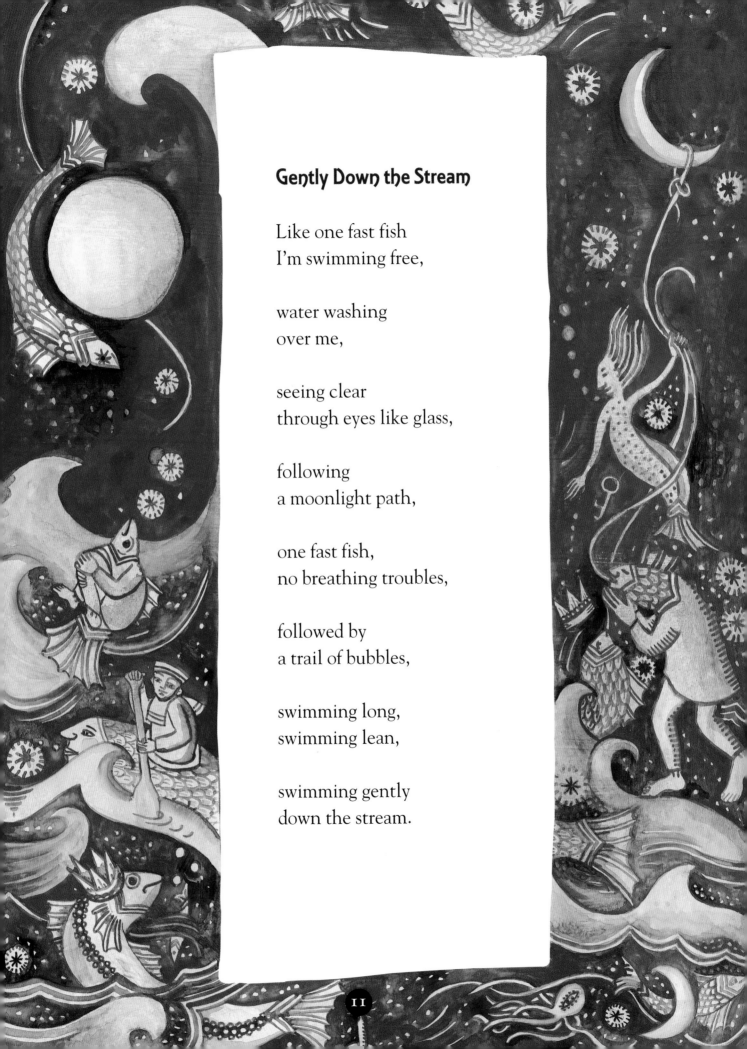

Gently Down the Stream

Like one fast fish
I'm swimming free,

water washing
over me,

seeing clear
through eyes like glass,

following
a moonlight path,

one fast fish,
no breathing troubles,

followed by
a trail of bubbles,

swimming long,
swimming lean,

swimming gently
down the stream.

Flying

In their dreams
my friends can fly.
They flap their arms
and soar like hawks.

I've never flown
except in planes.
I think I would be terrified
to find the ground lost
under me.
I like to go to sleep at nine,
curled up round
in my safe bed,
dreaming soft and fuzzy
things—

goose down dreams
cradling
my head.

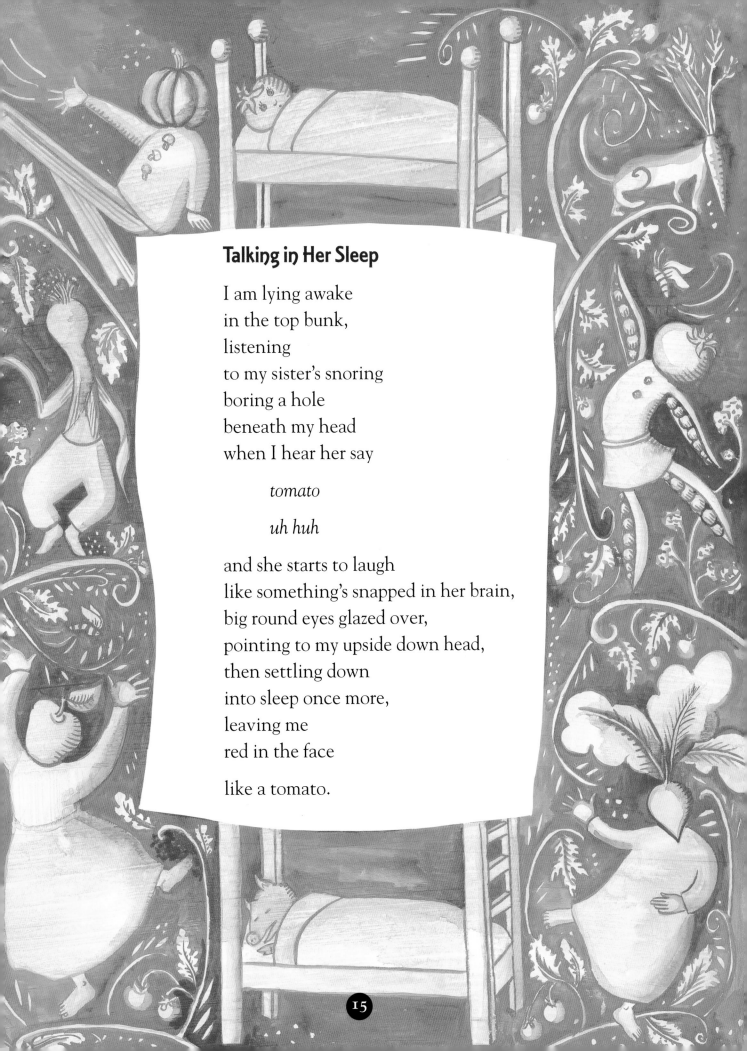

Talking in Her Sleep

I am lying awake
in the top bunk,
listening
to my sister's snoring
boring a hole
beneath my head
when I hear her say

  tomato

  uh huh

and she starts to laugh
like something's snapped in her brain,
big round eyes glazed over,
pointing to my upside down head,
then settling down
into sleep once more,
leaving me
red in the face

like a tomato.

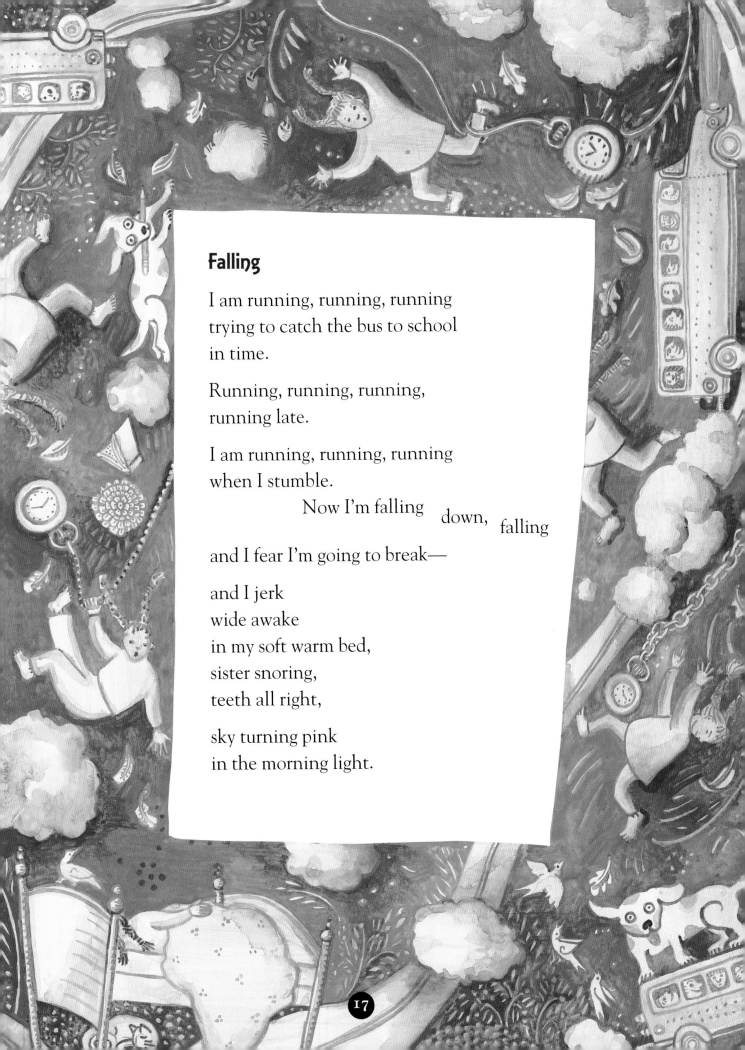

Falling

I am running, running, running
trying to catch the bus to school
in time.

Running, running, running,
running late.

I am running, running, running
when I stumble.
                Now I'm falling   down,   falling

and I fear I'm going to break—

and I jerk
wide awake
in my soft warm bed,
sister snoring,
teeth all right,

sky turning pink
in the morning light.

Dog Dreams

Our sad old dog
kicks his feet,
twitches, growls
in his sleep,
whimpers, snarls,
yelps awake.

I scratch
behind his ears
and take him out
to let him sniff
the trees,
let him walk,
chase the breeze,
nose in air,
eyes closed tight,
chasing dreams
into the night.

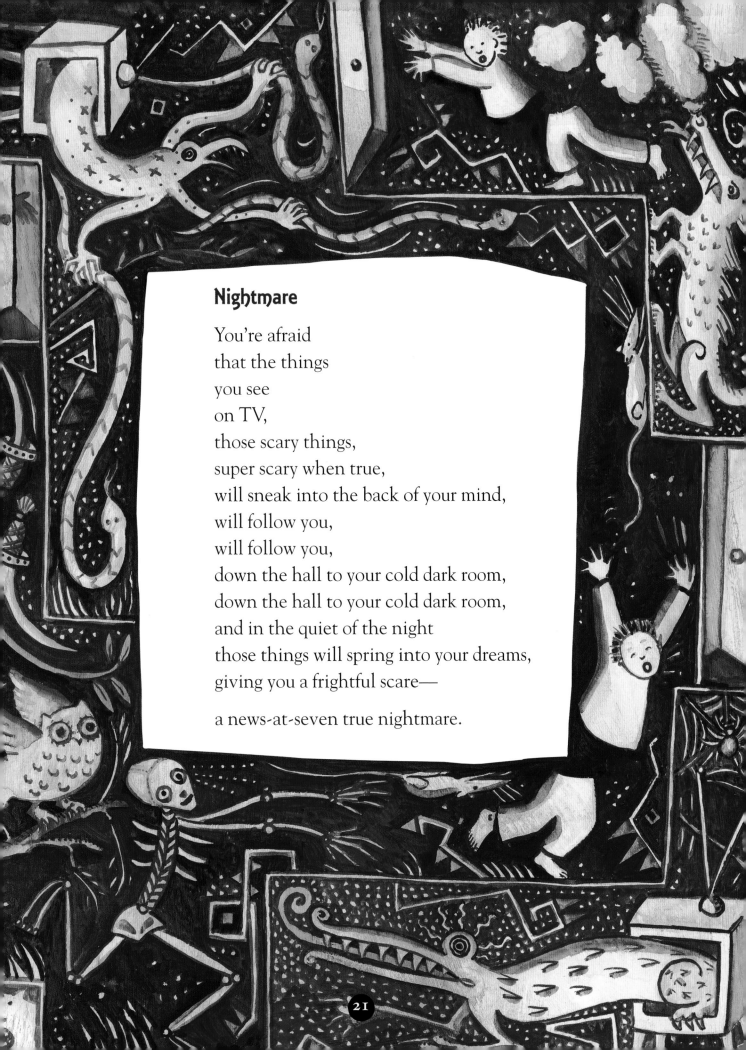

Nightmare

You're afraid
that the things
you see
on TV,
those scary things,
super scary when true,
will sneak into the back of your mind,
will follow you,
will follow you,
down the hall to your cold dark room,
down the hall to your cold dark room,
and in the quiet of the night
those things will spring into your dreams,
giving you a frightful scare—

a news-at-seven true nightmare.

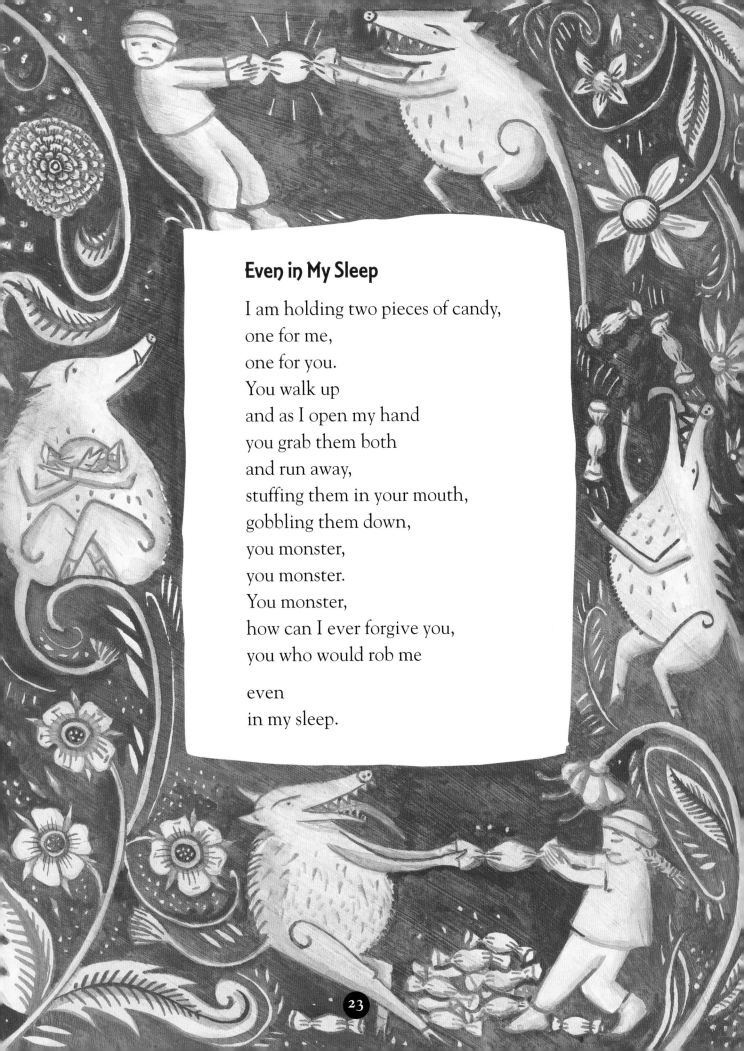

Even in My Sleep

I am holding two pieces of candy,
one for me,
one for you.
You walk up
and as I open my hand
you grab them both
and run away,
stuffing them in your mouth,
gobbling them down,
you monster,
you monster.
You monster,
how can I ever forgive you,
you who would rob me

even
in my sleep.

Turnip Cake

On the table
I find a slice of turnip cake,
its bits of color,
orange shrimp
and red sausage,
glowing almost
against the pale
mashed turnip.

The salt in it
bites the back of my mouth,
my soggy mouth,
watering over
this *lo bak go* like no other,
this *dim sum* of my dreams,
crisp to the teeth
and soft to the tongue,

and I wake up
hungry.

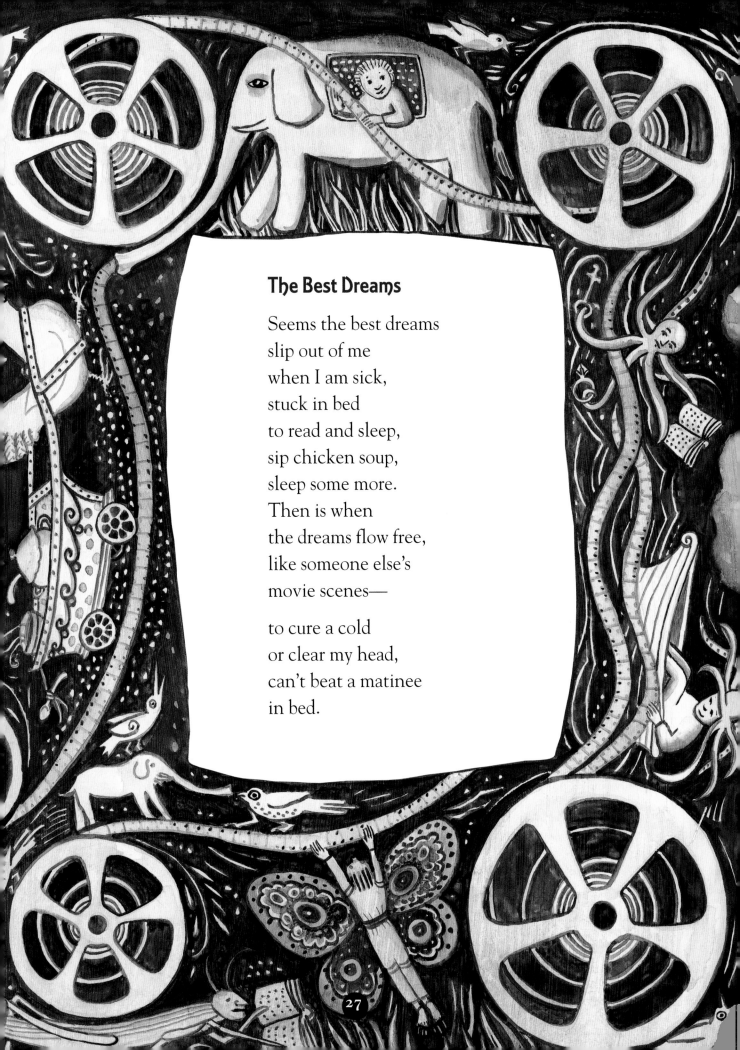

The Best Dreams

Seems the best dreams
slip out of me
when I am sick,
stuck in bed
to read and sleep,
sip chicken soup,
sleep some more.
Then is when
the dreams flow free,
like someone else's
movie scenes—

to cure a cold
or clear my head,
can't beat a matinee
in bed.

There Is a Place

There is a place

where the museum houses thousands of paintings
seen nowhere else in the world,
the colors so bright they grab your eyes
and hold you there, looking,

where the library is filled with brand new books
waiting for you to open them first,
to tell stories only you could know,

where fresh cherries have no pits,
where puppies never grow old.

There is such a place,
hidden deep
in me.